FLOWER GIRL FRIENDS

Sharla Scannell Whalen

Illustrations by
Taylor Bruce

ABDO & Daughters
Minneapolis

Published by Abdo & Daughters, 4940 Viking Drive, Suite 622, Edina, Minnesota 55435.

Printed in the United States.

Illustrations by Taylor Bruce

Edited by Laura Grieve and Ken Berg

Library of Congress Cataloging-in-Publication Data

Whalen, Sharla Scannell, 1960
     Flower girl friends / Sharla Scannell Whalen.
     p. cm.
     Summary: In the spring of 1897 on the Illinois prairie a teacher asks six students to be in her wedding.
     ISBN 1-56239-840-7
     [1. Teachers--Fiction. 2. Weddings--Fiction.] I. Title.
     PZ7.W5455F1 1997
     [Fic]--dc21   97-18184
                                         CIP
                                         AC

TABLE OF CONTENTS

CHAPTER ONE

SPRING!

After a long snowy winter, the first thaw came to the Illinois prairie in early March. Hannah Olson brushed her long brown hair out of her eyes, leaning from bed to reach the little window tucked under the eaves. She pushed it up an extra inch. Hannah had been awakened by the drip-dripping of the thaw. As she lay listening to the melting snow trickling off the roof, she heard the call of the first bird of spring. How had it known exactly when to come?

This was one morning she wasn't sorry that her mother had a rule about windows being kept open at night. It was healthful, her mother insisted, to let in a little fresh air while sleeping. With a bed near the window, Hannah sometimes had to burrow under the covers to keep warm; but she was glad it had been open *this* morning. Hannah felt as though she was part of the spring. She was hearing it arrive.

Hannah's mother entered her room with a load of freshly ironed laundry. "Good morning!" she said, kissing Hannah's forehead. "Wake up, Jennie," she called cheerfully to the little lump under the covers on the other bed. Mrs. Olson unlatched the blue and yellow doors of the gaily painted wardrobe to store the clean clothes.

"The snow is starting to melt, Mother! Perhaps Rachel and Matthew will be able to come out to Sunday dinner this week," Hannah said hopefully. Hannah's grown-up sister Rachel and her husband Matthew lived on a farm not far away, but the cold and bad roads had kept the two families apart a good deal.

"The fact is," Mrs. Olson began, "Rachel is now so far along, she will be spending most of her time at home." Rachel would be having a baby in just two more months. Hannah was very eager to meet her little niece or nephew. She hoped it would be a girl, but her mother reminded her that a healthy baby was all that mattered.

Everyone else at Cherry Hill Farm was anxious to greet the new season, too. But for the next several weeks, it always seemed temptingly close–but never arriving! Every minor thaw was followed by a hard freeze. The snow still stood a foot deep on field, garden, and lawn. But by now the surface was glazed, as though it had been coated with shiny sugar.

Yet, as March passed, the snowbanks began to shrink. The hard-pack on the road receded until they could see the brown dirt below. And one morning, Hannah spied the first patch of green grass. She had smiled as though greeting an old friend.

Hannah's older brother Aaron drove her to school in the wagon, for the road to Oakdale was three inches in mud.

Aaron always stopped at the little red house by the quarry to pick up Ellie Perry.

"My crocus bulbs are up!" Ellie proclaimed, climbing to join them on the high wagon seat. "I never expected to see those green spears poking right through the leftover snow. But Grandma says snow kept the bulbs warm through the winter, like a blanket. We had a layer of leaves raked over them, too."

"I'll have to go 'round to see what's sprouted at the farm," responded Hannah. "If the crocuses are here, the hyacinths won't be far behind."

"Grandma says I can have charge of the big flower bed on her front lawn–the one around the sundial," announced Ellie.

"Oh, your Grandma always has a beautiful garden there!" Hannah remembered. "I watched for it every time we drove up Quarry Road when I was little."

"Many of the flowers are perennials of course," said Ellie. "So they'll come up every year. It will be easy to take care of them. And it will be especially fun to select some seeds for the annuals."

"I'd like to help you plan that garden, Ellie. Working in the kitchen vegetable garden at home is a chore. But planting flowers would be a treat!"

Before school, Ellie and Hannah drew a plan for the garden. The flower bed was a large circle, with a planting of tiger lilies around the sundial. Ellie and Hannah decided to plant the annuals in rings around the center–the outermost circle being the lowest, with taller and taller varieties in each succeeding ring. The tiger lilies would be the tallest, in the center.

"Perhaps we could choose flowers that have had a special part in history. We could ask Miss Devine about it." Ellie was always interested in stories from history.

"What are you girls talking about?" demanded Maggie Sullivan, entering the classroom with her red braids swinging. She banged her books down on the adjacent desk then looked up sheepishly to smile an apology at their teacher. Frowning, Miss Devine shook her finger at Maggie, but there was a twinkle in her eye.

Maggie wasn't interested in gardening. She was full of news of her own. "Baseball practice starts this week. It will be my first chance to play a real season with the team. The few games we had last fall didn't count, really."

"I should say they did count!" Hannah exclaimed. "I'll never forget that game you pitched against Westbrook."

"You mean the one I almost *didn't* pitch against Westbrook! Well, that game wasn't part of the regular schedule, either. It was more for exhibition."

Beth Dunstable bustled into the classroom just before the bell rang. "The morning mail brought a set of spring fashion sheets from Mama in Paris. My, but the ladies will be wearing lovely things this spring. You should have seen the hats!"

"Hats!" repeated Maggie with disgust.

"Oh yes! I'd like one all done in peach and cream. Or perhaps a pistachio green hat would look better on blond hair. Can't you just picture it tied with a chocolate-brown ribbon?"

The girls giggled as Miss Devine rang her brass bell.

"Don't be in such a hurry to grow up, Beth!" whispered Ellie, grinning.

CHAPTER TWO

A RAINBOW IN THE OCTAGON

After classes one day, Miss Devine asked Maggie, Beth, Ellie, and Hannah if they would be baking that Saturday. The four had a business called "Best Bakers." They didn't work every weekend, but often enough to have built up a reputation for fine baked goods. This was due primarily to the excellent muffin recipes provided by Ellie's grandmother, as well as Maggie's mother–who knew the secret to making light and airy Irish scones.

"My Aunt Helen is having a small tea at Pine Craig Mansion on Saturday," Miss Devine explained. "She wondered if you could bring a dozen muffins. And we have another request. We'd like you to come to tea."

"Us?" Maggie blurted.

"That's right," Miss Devine said. "Please come to Pine Craig promptly at two o'clock. My aunt and I have something important to discuss with you."

As they skipped down the steps of the large brick school, the four girls saw Murgatroid Forsythe standing in the schoolyard. He was with Winifred Dore, a new girl in their class.

"Look Freddie," he grunted to Winifred. "The muffin-heads were kept after school."

Winifred giggled.

"Bet you're in trouble," Murg jeered at them.

"You're the one more likely to be in trouble," returned Ben Tarken, walking up with Daniel O'Leary.

"Come on Maggie, it's time for baseball practice," said Danny, with a dark glance for Murg.

Hannah looked at the other girls worriedly. "Do you suppose we *could* be in some sort of trouble?" she asked. "Is that why Miss Devine asked us to come to Pine Craig?"

"If we were, we wouldn't be invited to discuss it over tea!" snorted Maggie. The girls had grown accustomed to Maggie's brusque manner. She wasn't really being impolite, though people who didn't know her found her rather rough around the edges. Her observations could usually be more tactfully phrased, but they were always–as in this case–very much to the point.

Despite the obvious logic of Maggie's remark, the foursome felt a bit anxious. Early on Saturday, they gathered at Beth's house, which stood in elegance at the corner of Jefferson and Elm Streets. They were greeted as usual by Snowflake, Beth's fluffy white dog.

Agnes, the Dunstables' cook and housekeeper, always gave them the kitchen to themselves when they were baking. Gertie, the maid, supplied the girls with large coverall aprons. The Best Bakers usually wore the smaller gingham aprons Hannah's mother had made for them. But today the four were in their finest clothes, and Agnes wasn't going to let them take any chances.

"Taking tea at Pine Craig," Agnes said admiringly. "Very posh, indeed! You must look your best."

"I've never seen aprons with sleeves before," Ellie said, tying one on. She was wearing a taffeta dress in a fashionable shade of pale celery.

"Ellie," Beth admired, "Your dress is the very thing!"

"What thing?" asked Maggie, looking down at

her own dark green crushed velvet dress to straighten the ivory sash.

"The *latest* thing," explained Beth. "Ellie's wearing one of the new spring colors."

Ellie smiled. "I don't think Grandma knew that, when she helped me pick it out. Your dresses are all very fine, too, girls." She added, looking down at her small ruby-ring necklace, "We're all wearing our birthstones!"

For Beth's tenth birthday last fall, Mr. Dunstable had presented each of the girls with a birthstone ring. Until they were grown into, the rings were worn on thin gold chains.

Hannah's tiny green emerald gleamed against her dark maroon velvet dress, which was draped back to show a pink silk layer beneath. She was rather proud of the four tiers of lace she had helped her mother stitch around the bottom of the skirt.

Maggie's birthstone was a purple amethyst and Beth's a pinkish-yellow topaz. Beth was dressed in palest blue French silk, trimmed in white lace. Her mother, who lived in Paris, sent many of Beth's dresses.

The muffins, still warm from the oven, were placed evenly in a basket, then covered snugly

with a red and white striped cloth. The Best
Bakers untied their aprons, put on their hats, and
set out into the April sunshine for Pine Craig.

The carved front door had a large beveled
glass window in the top half. After Hannah had
rung the bell, the lace curtain behind the window
was pulled back, and the bright dark eyes of Miss
Devine's aunt twinkled out at them.

"Come in," she welcomed, swinging open the
door. "We've been expecting you!"

"Good afternoon, Mrs. Martin-Mitchell," the
girls said politely, stepping into the large foyer.

"We'll be taking tea in the Octagon," Mrs. Martin-Mitchell announced, leading the way.

"It looks so different without the snow!" Maggie observed.

The four friends had visited this eight-walled room last winter, after Beth's toboggan accident. The walls were all of glass, making the room seem like a greenhouse. It *did* look different without a wintery white view on every side.

Now the Octagon was surrounded by the sights of spring–the vivid green lawns stretching out to a copse of oak trees, with a wide border of tall yellow tulips and shorter grape hyacinths running along behind the house.

A large, round glass table in the center of the room held a pot of tea. Gold-rimmed cups on gold-rimmed saucers stood around the teapot. Miss Devine set the basket of muffins on the table and helped the young ladies to tea. They took mostly milk in their cups, with just a bit of tea "for color," Miss Devine winked.

"We've asked you here," Mrs. Martin-Mitchell said mysteriously, "to talk about a rainbow."

Mystified, the girls turned to Miss Devine.

"A rainbow wedding, that is," she added.

"A rainbow wedding!" Beth interrupted. "I've read about them in the society pages of the *Chicago Tribune*. Are you going to have a rainbow wedding, Miss Devine?"

"Yes, Beth," Miss Devine replied. "We thought it would be a lovely idea for a spring marriage."

"The bride will be all in white, of course," Mrs. Martin-Mitchell described. "But everything else will be in pastel rainbow shades–rose, peach, yellow, pale green, blue, and violet. The flowers and decorations will be done in these colors, as well as . . . the flower girls' gowns."

"Flower girls?" Ellie repeated.

"You girls make up something of a rainbow yourselves," Miss Devine smiled. "You're each very different, in appearance and in personality; yet your friendship is a beautiful blend. You were a natural choice for our rainbow wedding. If you are willing, that is."

The four friends looked at each other in wonder.

"If we're willing?!" shrieked Beth joyfully.

"I think we're willing," Maggie grinned.

CHAPTER

THREE

A WOMAN'S PLACE

Mr. Dunstable threw down the morning paper in disgust. Beth and Aunt Mary looked up with surprise from their oatmeal.

"It's this editorial in the *Oakdale Observer*," he explained. "The headline says, 'A Woman's Place is in the Home.' What really gets my goat is that this fellow is really writing about Miss Devine being retained as teacher at Oakdale School after her marriage. But he doesn't have the nerve to say so. Just goes on about how married women oughtn't have careers. Doesn't he know it's 1897? Things are changing, but this fellow wants to hide his head in the sand."

"Poor Miss Devine!" cried Beth. "How must this make her feel?"

"If she's a sensible woman–as I have no doubt that she is–she'll ignore it," Aunt Mary concluded stiffly.

Nevertheless, Beth was eager to reach school that morning. She was glad that Hannah, Ellie, and Maggie were prompt, too. Beth told them about the editorial. Arriving in the classroom, Polly Sanders said her father had spoken of it at their breakfast table, too. He thought there was something to the writer's point of view. Polly's mother said she wasn't sure.

By the time classes began, those who *had* heard about the letter in the paper had told those who hadn't, and the room was buzzing.

Miss Devine jingled her brass bell to call the class to order. She looked a little pale.

"I can see that you've heard about the editorial in the paper. Perhaps it would be best for me to explain, for those of you who don't understand.

"There are people who believe that women, particularly married women, should not be permitted to undertake careers. It has been a tradition for women who teach school, in particular, to retire after they are married. Most school boards, even in big cities, will not hire a married woman.

"Mr. Moore and I feel that this is wrong."

Miss Devine pushed back a strand of curly golden brown which had come loose from the thick braided bun at the back of her head. "There are many women who struck out for themselves and made a success. Why, there's Mrs. Belva Lockwood. She was the first woman lawyer to present a case before the Supreme Court of the United States. And there's Nellie Bly. Have you heard her name?"

Beth's hand went up. "Nellie Bly is a newspaper reporter."

"That's right, " Miss Devine nodded. "She set out to break the record of Jules Verne who traveled around the world in 80 days. Nellie made it in 72 days!

"And don't forget about Dr. Mary Walker. Not only did she practice medicine, but she served as an officer in the Civil War. There's a picture of her in this magazine," said Miss Devine, holding it up. "Dr. Walker has been known to go out in public in gentlemen's pants, frock coat, and high silk hat."

"Do you want to wear trousers, Miss Devine?" asked Aidan Sullivan, Maggie's younger brother.

"No, Aidan," Miss Devine smiled. "Dr. Walker was just trying to make a point. She was saying that women ought not be prevented from doing the same things men do. These women may never be famous, but they'll take their place in history. They are paving the way for change. This kind of change takes a very long time, but it will come. Have you heard about the rights-for-women movement?"

"I've heard my ma and pa arguing about whether women ought to be allowed to vote," Ben Tarken answered.

"Women had the right to vote in Wyoming Territory by 1869," Miss Devine said. "And they'll have it in all 45 states one day. It may not be in my lifetime, but I hope it will be in yours.

"My contribution to all this is very simple. As you know, last winter Mr. Moore and I went to the school board and explained that we would be getting married. We asked that the board consider allowing me to continue teaching."

"Did you tell them about Nellie Bly and the doctor who wears pants?" asked Danny O'Leary.

"Yes, I did," Miss Devine laughed.

"We're certainly glad they agreed to let you keep your job, Miss Devine," sighed Ellie.

"So am I," finished Miss Devine. "But there are folks who don't feel the same way. They are entitled to their opinion."

Miss Devine hadn't noticed Mr. Moore step quietly into the room. He was standing at her elbow. "If you ask me," he finally spoke, "a woman's place . . . is anywhere she cares to go!"

CHAPTER
FOUR

MADAME COLETTE'S

The next day after dismissal, Hannah lingered in the classroom.

"I have a question, Miss Devine," she said.

"You do look serious, Hannah. Is there a problem?"

"Not a problem," Hannah ruminated. "Just something I was thinking about. Mrs. Martin-Mitchell named six shades for the rainbow wedding. But aren't there seven colors in the rainbow?"

Miss Devine laughed in agreement. "You're quite a scientist, Hannah! And you're absolutely right. There are seven colors in the spectrum. The missing one is indigo. It's between dark blue and grayish purple. Since we'll be using pastel shades of each color, we're leaving indigo out. Besides, I'm not sure we could find you a dress in 'pale indigo'!"

"That's another question I have. You're using six shades of the rainbow, but there are only four of us girls."

"You must have been reading my mind. I've been thinking the very same thing. I intend to ask Polly Sanders to join the wedding party. She is so shy and quiet, I think it will draw her out and do her good. And what would you think of Winifred Dore as the sixth flower girl?"

"The new girl?" Hannah asked drawing out the question.

"She doesn't seem to have made any friends yet. It would be nice for her to get to know you girls this way. You can start getting to know one another better on Saturday. I'll be sending notes home to your parents tomorrow to ask if you may join us in Chicago for a dress fitting."

The other girls were happy to hear that Polly would be a flower girl, too. But they were surprised when Hannah told them about Winifred.

"Isn't she Murg's pal?" Maggie asked with distaste.

"I don't really think so," said Ellie thoughtfully. "He may want her to be his friend, but I don't know that she is."

Saturday proved very eventful. No baking was done. Instead, the four girls and Beth's Aunt Mary met Miss Devine and her aunt at the train station. Polly and Winifred were there, too. They were thrilled to be going into Chicago to be sized for their rainbow dresses.

"There's been something I've been wanting to say to you girls," Winifred said quietly. "I'm sorry I laughed when Murg called you names. I wasn't trying to be rude. It just sounded funny."

"That's okay," Beth reassured her.

"We're glad you explained, Winifred," Hannah said.

"Call me Winnie," she rejoined.

"Not Freddie?" asked Maggie.

"No," Winnie said. "That was Murg's idea. My family always calls me Winnie."

Out on the platform, the girls chattered in their excitement. Mrs. Martin-Mitchell pointed to an advertisement on the platform wall. "Look who's coming to Chicago."

The friends turned to look. Beth and Maggie stood transfixed, eyes riveted on the poster.

"Buffalo Bill," murmured Maggie.

"Look at those horses," whispered Beth.

"The Show of Shows," Maggie continued.

"The Race of Races," Beth added.

"What are you two talking about?" asked Ellie.

Beth and Maggie seemed to come out of a trance. "Papa said over 40,000 people went to see his show the last time Buffalo Bill was here," Beth related. "Aunt Mary thought I was too young. But I can go this time, can't I, Auntie?"

"We'll speak to your father, Beth," Aunt Mary responded dourly.

"I have got to see that show," said Maggie reverently. "I've simply *got* to!"

"Maybe we can all go," suggested Ellie.

"It looks like quite a show." Hannah gazed up at the poster. "Look at those Rough Riders!"

"Perhaps you'll see more billboards for the show in Chicago," said Miss Devine. "Here comes the train."

Beth rode the rails every week to take her lesson at Sommerfield Riding Academy, but it was a novelty to the other girls.

"Do you think the engineer will highball?" Maggie asked.

"What does that mean?" wondered Hannah.

"Maggie is wondering if the engineer will

attempt to achieve a dangerously high speed in order to travel the distance to Chicago in record time," explained Aunt Mary.

"That won't happen today, Maggie," said Miss Devine. "This train makes several stops. Hinsdale will be the first one, I think."

In just over an hour, the locomotive was pulling into Chicago's Union Station. Mrs. Martin-Mitchell led the way through the noisy crowd of departing and arriving passengers, with Miss Devine bringing up the rear. Aunt Mary hovered around the children protectively.

The girls craned their necks to stare at the colorful advertisements for Buffalo Bill's Wild West show displayed throughout the station and out on State Street. One showed Annie Oakley, another a group of Rough Riders.

"You girls only have eyes for Buffalo Bill!" Aunt Mary complained. "When you look around Chicago, you should think of the Phoenix."

"What is the Phoenix, Miss Dunstable?" Ellie asked.

"It's a bird," Aunt Mary answered.

"According to Egyptian mythology, it could rise from its own ashes," Miss Devine told them.

"You could think of Chicago that way."

"I should say so!" exclaimed Aunt Mary. "You children have all heard of the Great Chicago Fire. In little more than twenty-five years, this town grew from a burned wasteland into the resplendent city it is today."

"The fire happened in the fall of 1871," Miss Devine picked up the story. "There had been no rain for weeks and the city was dry as tinder. The fire broke out in the Irish section of town, in Mrs. O'Leary's barn."

"Do you think she was related to Danny?" Maggie whispered. Ellie nudged her to be quiet.

"The fire swept through the shanties, blazing higher and higher," continued Miss Devine. "Since most of the city's buildings were pine, the flames destroyed everything in their path. It burned over 2,000 acres clear to the ground."

"Chicago roared back to life," Mrs. Martin-Mitchell said, "and with buildings of masonry and metal, instead of pine. The new Chicago was the birthplace of the skyscraper. The first one went up here a decade ago. And now there are many Chicago buildings which scrape the sky. Some have ten stories or more."

The girls looked at the beautiful buildings up and down State Street. It was hard to imagine the gleaming city as a pile of ash.

Mrs. Martin-Mitchell led the way to Madame Colette's Fine Dressmaking Shop on State Street. They were greeted by Madame herself, who led them into a large room with walls of sky blue.

Madame Colette clapped her hands, and several young women came in carrying bolts of fabric. They unrolled the lovely shades of organza, which seemed almost to float.

"Look, Delia," Mrs. Martin-Mitchell pointed out, "how the violet suits Hannah."

"Violet has always looked good on *me*," whispered Winnie to Polly.

"And Beth has always looked very prepossessing in pink," remarked Aunt Mary.

"Does that mean she *likes* you in pink?" whispered Winnie to Beth. Smiling, Beth nodded.

"What about the peach for me?" asked Winnie, holding the fabric in front of herself.

"Fine, Winnie," agreed Miss Devine. "It's very flattering to you."

"Mademoiselle Polly's honey blond hair is set off well by the sky blue, I think," offered Madame Colette.

"Ellie looks lovely in the soft yellow," said Miss Devine.

"And the mint green is just right against Maggie's beautiful red curls," concluded Mrs. Martin-Mitchell.

Miss Devine stepped back and surveyed them with satisfaction. "Well, I guess that's the six of you. You are going to be a beautiful rainbow!"

After measuring the girls, Madame Colette took Miss Devine and her aunt into another room for a fitting of the wedding dress. The girls enjoyed fruit and frosty glasses of ice water while they waited.

On the stroll back to the station, the girls forgot about weddings and dresses. They fell once again under the spell of the Buffalo Bill posters. Maggie and Beth talked about the wonders of the Wild West Show all the way home.

CHAPTER

FIVE

MAY DAY

It wasn't long before all the children at school knew that Buffalo Bill Cody was bringing his Wild West Show to Chicago. Many of them hoped to attend, including all four girls.

"The tickets cost fifty cents each!" cautioned Ellie.

"But remember, we're businesswomen," Maggie said. "Let's get baking!"

Talk at school was dominated by Buffalo Bill, so much that Miss Devine had to call the attention back to the project the class had been working on.

The children had been very busy preparing for May Day. The first day of May was always special in Oakdale, as it was also the annual celebration of the founding of the town. There would be speeches at the new courthouse which was now fully functional–the records having been procured from Westbrook several months previous. And there would be recitations and presentations by the children of the school. Each class was responsible for part of the program.

Mr. Moore was directing the upper grades in creating tableaux of the history of Oakdale from 1830 to the present. The first would show the arrival of Joseph Oake and his family to this lovely spot on the DuPage River.

Miss Devine's class would be responsible for the Maypole dance. This represented the celebration of modern, 1890s Oakdale and its hopes for the next century–just a few years away.

Mr. Beebe at the dry goods shop had donated remnants of fabric, which Miss Devine's class had cut into strips. Each child made his or her own streamer, sewing the narrow strips together, end-to-end. They would be attached to the flagpole in front of the courthouse. For one day, the flagpole would be converted to a Maypole, and the American flag would be moved to the top of the courthouse tower.

Most of the girls in the class chose calico fabric for their streamers. Beth chose pink, of course, with a pattern of tiny yellow flowers. Maggie picked green fabric with tiny white daisies, while Ellie found a solid yellow. Hannah and Ben both settled on red. Hers was red calico with tiny, yellow star-shaped flowers, while his was a red checked flannel. The most unusual streamer was that brought by Murg Forsythe. He had cut it out of black crepe fabric.

"A black streamer, Murg?" questioned Miss Devine.

"You said we could choose anything we liked ... or bring in fabric from home. That's what I did."

"You're right. The choice is yours. I just thought that black might look a little odd among all the brightly colored streamers."

"That's all right," said Murg. He smiled as though he liked the idea of looking odd.

§

There were no classes on May Day. The program would begin at nine o'clock sharp. Many of the children and parents joined the teachers at sunrise to prepare. The older children began assembling the tableaux of Oakdale's history. These scenes would be presented one at a time on the porch of the courthouse, which would be their stage.

Mr. Dunstable was attaching streamers to the Maypole. Mrs. Olson and several other mothers helped hand streamers to Mr. Dunstable, who was high atop a ladder.

Pulling Murg's black streamer from the pile, Mrs. Olson expressed surprised. "Does this belong here?" she asked Miss Devine.

"Yes," Miss Devine answered. "I told the children they could pick the fabric for their ribbons. And that was Murg's choice." Miss Devine smiled and gave a little shrug.

"It takes all kinds to make a world," said Mrs. Olson philosophically, passing the black streamer up to Mr. Dunstable.

"This is cheerful," he remarked with a wry look.

"How is Rachel feeling?" asked Mrs. Sullivan, passing a streamer to Mrs. Olson.

"She'll be glad when May is over, I'll say that!" Mrs. Olson exclaimed.

When the pole was assembled, Miss Devine called the children together for a rehearsal. They had practiced on a pole with plain rope "streamers" in the schoolyard, so that Miss Devine could teach them the interweaving steps of the dance. But the flagpole at the courthouse was much higher. "I'm glad we're going to have a chance to try it out here," Hannah said, tucking apple blossoms into

her brown braid. All the girls had flowers in their hair.

"Oh, we won't have any problems," Murg Forsythe responded. "We know what to do. Don't we, Freddie?"

Winnie Dore looked at him and frowned.

The longer streamers and taller pole provided no difficulties, until Murg Forsythe took a wrong turn, entangling all of them.

"He did that on purpose," Maggie hissed indignantly.

"You went the opposite way, Murg," Miss Devine pointed out. "You never had any problems with this before. Shall we try it again?"

"No, Miss Devine," Murg said. "I'll be careful."

"It would be just like him to try to ruin the Maypole dance," Beth said under her breath.

The May Day-Founders' Day Program began with speeches by the mayor and Judge Cody. Mr. Forsythe, who worked in the mayor's office, also spoke. This was Murg's uncle. Mr. Forsythe told a story about his grandfather's arrival in Oakdale not many years after the founding of the town. "And I'm proud to announce that, this summer,

Oakdale will be dedicating a statue to my grandfather, Simon Forsythe."

Beth looked sharply up at her father. She had understood that the statue planned for Oakdale's Central park would be dedicated to her own great-grandfather, Henry Dunstable. He had died long before she was born, but she loved to hear stories about his colorful life.

Mr. Dunstable, sitting in the sunny front row with the other Town Council members, frowned slightly at Mr. Forsythe's announcement. But he smiled as he rose to speak about plans for the future of Oakdale.

Maggie elbowed Ellie. "Look over there," she said.

Winnie was holding Murg by the arm and whispering earnestly into his ear. At last, he nodded grudging agreement to whatever she was saying.

The youngest children in Oakdale School were the first to perform in the program. Accompanied by the high school band, they sang "The Star-Spangled Banner" and received enthusiastic applause.

The Maypole dance came next. The band

played a rousing song and the children in Miss Devine's class stepped lively. The girls were relieved that it came off without a hitch and wondered if they had Winnie to thank.

Green curtains had been hung across the front of the courthouse porch. Ben had been recruited to present the titles of the tableaux, written on large placards. He stood beside an easel to one side. At a signal from behind the curtain, Ben placed a large card on the easel. "The Birth of Oakdale," it read.

The curtains were drawn back to reveal a Conestoga wagon–made in Joseph Oake's hometown in Lancaster County, Pennsylvania. He came west with his wife and six children in 1830. Children in the upper grades were dressed as Joseph Oake and his children. They weren't supposed to move during the tableau, and they looked as still as wax figures. The audience politely refrained from laughing when "Mr. Oake's" hat fell over his eyes.

The curtains were closed, and the audience clapped. Then the band played a quiet tune while the next scenes were set up.

They represented such moments as the opening of Joe Oake's general store, the establishment of the Oakdale Post Office and the first bank, the departure of local men to regiments in the Civil War, and the arrival of the railroad in Oakdale.

At last Ben was putting up the final placard. He was looking at the four friends with a twinkle in his eye. "The Rightful Return of the County Records," the little sign read. When the curtains were drawn, the scene showed a wagon loaded with barrels and cartons. Boys were frozen in the act of bringing boxes of record books to the wagon. And peeking over the edge of the wagon box were four pairs of frightened eyes.

"That's supposed to be us," Ellie whispered to the others. The audience voiced uproarious approval at this last tableau, and many turned to smile at the four heroines of current-day Oakdale. They were both embarrassed and honored to have been included in the pageant.

"I guess we really are a part of Oakdale history," said Maggie in an awed voice.

CHAPTER

SIX

BUTTONS, BAKING, AND BUFFALO BILL

The four girls had only one baking day left before the Buffalo Bill show. They had taken orders for scones that week and did their baking at Maggie's house.

The Best Bakers had regular customers, eliminating the need to sell door-to-door. Orders were sometimes relayed through Mrs. McGuire at her store. The girls often stopped there after school.

"Mrs. Beebe would like a dozen scones on Saturday," Mrs. McGuire told them today.

"Thank you for taking the message, Mrs. McGuire," said Beth.

"It's my pleasure. Always good to see other women succeed in business," Mrs. McGuire winked. "Now then, have you come in to look at the new buttons?" The friends had button collections to which they regularly made additions.

"Oh, look at those little heart-shaped buttons!" cried Beth.

"They're beautiful," agreed Hannah. "But we've come for a packet of currants. We're going to make scones and buns tomorrow, Mrs. McGuire."

"That sounds yummy. Would you put Mr. McGuire and me down for half a dozen currant buns?"

"Certainly," nodded Ellie, pulling back out the notebook into which she had noted Mrs. Beebe's request a few minutes earlier. Ellie always recorded their customers' names and the orders they received. Hannah, who kept careful track of the Best Bakers' finances, paid Mrs. McGuire.

"Thank you, we'll see you tomorrow," Maggie called out as the foursome went back to Main Street.

Hannah and Ellie walked home together as usual, out west on Quarry Road. They spent a half hour each day working on the sundial garden at Ellie's.

It felt good to be digging in the warm soil again, helping things grow.

"Gardening makes me think of my mother," said Ellie pensively. Hannah looked up at this unexpected remark. Ellie almost never mentioned her mother. It had been less than two years since she died, and

Hannah supposed it hurt for Ellie to talk about.

Hannah was correct. Grandma Perry often reminisced about happy memories of Ellie's mother. Listening to her grandmother made Ellie feel good, but it was too painful for her to bring up the subject herself. Working in the garden, Ellie felt close to her mother, who had loved flowers, too. Ellie told Hannah about a multicolored pansy patch her mother had designed one spring when they were living in Kentucky.

After her mother had died there, Reverend Perry had transferred to a Chicago church and Ellie had come to live with her grandmother in Oakdale. He came to visit as often as he could.

Ellie brushed loose dirt from her maroon checked skirts and sighed, "Think how beautiful this garden will look by summer."

"Next week maybe we'll get to the snapdragons," said Hannah. "I wish I could stay longer, but I'd better get home. Aaron and Joshua will be driving into town first thing tomorrow. They'll take us out to Maggie's. See you in the morning!"

The next day was so warm and so lovely, Hannah and Ellie, sitting together in the back of the Olson wagon, preferred spending it gardening rather than baking. But they did look forward to spending a morning with their friends, and they always enjoyed a visit to Maggie's house.

"Welcome," said six-year-old Aidan in a mysterious-sounding voice. He and his twin, Brigid, had been watching for the girls at the front door. "A powerful magic potion is being concocted in the kitchen," Aidan intoned.

"And they're going to put in some eye of newt," added Brigid.

"Brigid Mary Sullivan!" laughed Maggie's mother. "You know very well those are currants. They're no different from raisins. Eye of newt, indeed!"

"So Brigid knows what eye of newt looks like." Aidan was hatching a plot, as usual. "What kind of company do you keep on Halloween night after the rest of us are asleep?"

"What have you been reading, Aidan?" Ellie asked.

"Macbeth," he replied promptly.

"Is he really reading Shakespeare, Mrs. Sullivan?" asked Hannah.

"Well, I've been reading some to him," Maggie's mother explained. "Of course, I have to skip over a good bit. Yet he loves the stories and is always after me to read him the exciting ones."

"Macbeth is *very* exciting," Aidan said emphatically. "But you skip too much, Mother."

Hannah and Ellie chuckled as they made their way through the front parlor, waving at little Daisy who had her paperdolls spread out across the floor.

"Where's the eye of newt?" asked Ellie. Beth and Maggie looked up from the kitchen table.

"You've been talking to Brigid," observed Maggie dryly.

"Here it is," giggled Beth, pointing to a pile of freshly washed currants. "Mrs. Sullivan said we should put them into some sugar water to soak while we mix up the batter. They'll be less sour that way."

Aidan and Brigid were peeking around the kitchen door as Beth began dropping currants into a bowl. "Look!" whispered Brigid. "They're making eye of newt *soup*."

"Mother!" cried Maggie. "The twins won't let us work!"

"Go along, little ones," chuckled Mrs. Sullivan, coming in. "Now, Hannah. Tell us how your sister is doing." Maggie's mother was always interested in babies.

"We were out to see Rachel and Matthew last Sunday," answered Hannah. "And Rachel is . . . large!"

"Well, she's getting very close to her time. You'll be an aunt by the end of the month."

"Mother!" came Daisy's little voice from the parlor. "The twins won't let me work!"

Laughing, Mrs. Sullivan went to rescue Daisy.

The Best Bakers made two batches of scones and two of currant buns. Packing them carefully into clean cloths, the girls loaded their baskets and set out to make deliveries.

By the time they were finished, the four were tired but pleased. They now had earned enough for the fifty-cent tickets to the Wild West Show.

"Buffalo Bill, here we come!" said Maggie.

The big day finally arrived. The four girls had an early lunch and met at the train station. Joshua and Kevin generously agreed to act as chaperones and treated the group to train fare.

Beth and Maggie could hardly keep still for the train ride. They fairly bounced in their seats the whole trip. Kevin and Joshua egged them on.

"Do you suppose Annie Oakley will be there?" asked Kevin.

"They call her 'Little Sure Shot,' " said Maggie.

"Did you know that Buffalo Bill used to ride the Pony Express?" questioned Joshua.

"I believe the show begins with a parade of a band on horseback," remarked Kevin.

Maggie and Beth by then were standing, applauding the prospect.

The arena was brilliantly lit, and there were so many things happening that the girls hardly knew which way to look.

Maggie pulled a package of gum from her pinafore pocket and offered some to the others, as they watched displays of fancy roping tricks and deadeye marksmanship. She was speechless as she stared at Buffalo Bill himself, and almost stopped chewing her gum! Riding at full tilt, Bill fired his rifle and hit dozens of small glass balls.

Beth couldn't take her eyes off the Rough Riders. "They're the best horsemen in the world. And they're riding the finest horses in the world," she said reverently to Hannah.

Both Hannah and Ellie heartily enjoyed watching their friends' enthusiasm. On the ride home, they smiled as they observed the dreamy looks on the faces of Beth and Maggie. Occasionally, Beth muttered

something about the horses in the show. Maggie came out of her trance to ask, "If I met him, do you suppose I could call him "Bill'? Or would 'Mr. Cody' be more respectful?"

Kevin and Joshua laughed.

"What did I say?" demanded Maggie.

"Nothing, Sis," said Kevin. "We're just glad you enjoyed the show so much!"

CHAPTER SEVEN

HANNAH'S BIRTHDAY SURPRISE

"May 16th was a nice day to be born," thought Hannah on the morning of her birthday. It was another bright, sunny day. Perhaps she could go out to Ellie's and work on their garden. Then Ellie could come back to Cherry Hill Farm late in the afternoon for Hannah's birthday celebration.

It was to be a small party this year . . . just the four friends. "We'll keep it simple," Mrs. Olson had planned. Hannah knew her mother was worried about Rachel and the baby, who would soon be arriving.

Mrs. Olson was silent at breakfast. "Hannah, dear," she began at last, "We're not going to be able to have a party here today. But your brother Aaron rode out to talk to Mrs. Perry, and she said you may have a birthday picnic at Ellie's house."

"But Mother . . ." Hannah began.

"I'll explain later, Hannah. Don't worry. But don't ask me about it now. Help Jennie get ready. Joshua is going to take her to play with Daisy Sullivan."

It was difficult not to ask what was going on. But Hannah obediently put on her bonnet and helped Jennie tie hers.

Joshua was reassuring as he helped the girls up into the wagon.

"Well, I guess I got my wish," thought Hannah as they arrived at Ellie's little red house. "I *was* hoping to work on the garden today."

Hannah went through the little gate in the white picket fence to find Ellie under the big oak tree, playing with her cat, Cleo. "Hello!" Ellie waved gaily.

"Have fun, girls," Joshua called out. "I'll drop off Jennie and bring Maggie and Beth back here with me. See you soon."

"Lots of mysteries!" Ellie reported. "Grandma says we can't come into the house this morning."

"We can't go inside?" Hannah repeated.

"Grandma wouldn't say why. But there's lots to do out here," Ellie answered, nodding her head towards the sundial garden on the other side of the little yard.

"Let's get started," Hannah suggested. The two girls worked steadily in the garden until they heard wagon wheels approaching. They were expecting to see Joshua.

"Papa!" Ellie cried, as Reverend Perry pulled his buggy up to the little gate. He climbed down to give his daughter a hug.

"We finished painting the church hall ahead of schedule," Reverend Perry smiled. He was the pastor of a busy congregation in Chicago and spent the better part of every week there.

Ellie missed her father very much, but understood why he felt she was better off living with her grandmother. Ellie had traveled with him from church to church for the first nine years of her life, and he felt it was time for her to "settle down." She still liked to visit the church, but she couldn't think of a nicer place to be than at her grandmother's cozy house.

"We're having a birthday party here today, Papa," Ellie informed him.

"That's wonderful," he said. "Save a piece of cake for me. Let me get Star unhitched. She must be thirsty." He drove his buggy around back to the little buggy shed.

Ellie darted a glance at Hannah, who looked a trifle sad. There wouldn't be any birthday cake.

Just then, Joshua returned with Maggie and Beth.

They tumbled out of the wagon and shouted "Thank you!" as Hannah's brother rolled on towards Cherry Hill Farm.

"Guess who we saw in town!" commanded Maggie.

"Winnie–or should I say Freddie," Beth told them. "She was walking along Main Street with Murg Forsythe. I can't figure her out. Why does she even talk to him? Yuck!"

"I don't think she likes him," said Hannah. "But she seems to be having trouble telling him to leave her alone."

"Your garden looks beautiful," admired Beth. "And you chose my favorite color for the outside border. What pretty pink flowers."

"They're called impatiens. We grew them from seeds on Ellie's window seat," Hannah said.

"I'm getting kind of 'impatien' myself," Maggie joked. "When's lunch?"

Grandma Perry came out to the porch again to greet Maggie and Beth. "Ellie and Maggie," she directed, "you two come help carry out the food. Beth, you can be in charge of arranging the picnic cloth. And Hannah, come over here for a moment."

From behind her back, Grandma Perry presented a wreath of flowers and placed in on Hannah's head.

"You're the birthday girl, Hannah. So you're queen for the day. You may sit under the oak tree and give orders."

Hannah giggled. "Thank you for the wreath," she told Mrs. Perry. "It's so pretty!"

Sitting under the tree, Ellie whispered to Hannah, "*That's* the secret she was working on in the house!"

Beth arranged a blue and white checked picnic cloth under the tree. She set a small plate at each corner with a fork and spoon.

Maggie set down a bowl of coleslaw and a glass tray of dill pickles cut in spears. Ellie carried out a plate of miniature open-faced sandwiches, topped with sprigs of parsley. "There are two kinds," she said. "Chicken salad on rye and cream cheese on pumpernickel."

"Yum!" Maggie rubbed her stomach. "I'll try them both!"

"You know," mused Beth, munching on a pickle, "Now that Hannah's birthday has come, I think it's time to start counting down the days before *my* birthday."

"But Beth," objected Ellie. "Your birthday is six months away!"

"And I seem to recall your promising to wait to

start the countdown until your birthday is fewer than one hundred days away," Maggie reminded.

"All right," Beth agreed. "I'll wait. But I do love birthdays! Ellie's is next."

"The Fourth of July is a very patriotic day for a birthday," observed Hannah.

As they finished lunch, Hannah surveyed the lovely picnic scene and at the tidy yard surrounded by its white picket fence. Hannah thought it had been a wonderful birthday. But there was one more surprise. She saw Grandma Perry coming out the front door. Ten candles were glowing on . . . a giant muffin!

The friends were laughing so hard, they could hardly sing "Happy Birthday to You," which Grandma Perry had begun. They'd never seen such a giant muffin.

"It's your favorite," Grandma Perry announced. "Banana with chocolate pieces baked right in. And wait till you see how big the chocolate pieces are!"

But before Hannah could even blow out the candles, they heard a wagon approaching, fast. A big cloud of dust had been kicked up. And off of it jumped Joshua. He ran up to the picket fence and leaned against it, panting.

"Wait till you hear about your birthday present,

Hannah!" he exclaimed. "You're an aunt!"

"I'm an aunt!" shrieked Hannah, jumping up and down, knocking off her flower wreath. "What is it?!"

"It's a baby," Joshua teased.

"Joshua," protested Hannah. "Tell me!"

"Okay. It's a baby . . . girl," he smiled.

Hannah sank back down under the tree. "A girl," she sighed, grinning.

"I'm to bring you right out to their farm, Hannah," Joshua told her. "Rachel wants to see you."

"Joshua, if you have time to eat a piece of muffin-cake, I'll be able to wrap up a pair of booties I knitted for the little one," Grandma Perry said. "And Hannah, you'd better blow out these candles. Quick!"

Hannah made a hasty wish and blew out the candles with one deep puff. Beth helped serve pieces of the muffin cake, which was delicious. Grandma Perry came out shortly with a little packet tied with pink ribbon. "Pink booties," she remarked, putting them into Hannah's hands, "for the baby's birthday."

"That's right," Hannah realized. "It's the

baby's birthday, too! But how did you know to knit *pink* booties?"

"I knit a blue pair, too–just in case," winked Grandma Perry.

§

Hannah's excitment mounted on the ride to Rachel and Matthew's home, Applewood Farm. Her mother was sitting in a rocker on the front porch as they drove up to the farmhouse. Mrs. Olson appeared tired but very happy.

"Rachel's been waiting for the birthday girl," she told them.

"Which one?" laughed Joshua.

"*My* birthday girl," said Mrs. Olson, giving Hannah a hug. "Go on in and see the other birthday girl."

Hannah and Joshua tiptoed into the bedroom, followed by their mother. Matthew, beaming with pride, was sitting in a rocking chair by the window, holding a bundle wrapped in pink. Rachel was sitting up in bed, lace-trimmed pillows at her back. She was beaming, too, and looking radiant and pleased.

"Don't you want an introduction your niece?" Matthew asked Hannah. Now that the moment had come, Hannah was nervous.

Hannah approached the window anxiously, as Matthew drew the pink blanket from the baby's face. Hannah leaned down to look. The baby's face was like a rose. She was perfect. Her skin looked soft as silk, and Hannah breathed in a faint sweet baby-scent. The baby's tiny pink mouth curved in a little smile. "What can she be dreaming of," Hannah wondered.

As though the baby had heard her, the tiny almond-shaped eyes opened slowly and looked right up into Hannah's. "I thought babies were blind when they were born," said Hannah softly. "But she can see me. I know she can!"

"I'm sure you're right," observed Mrs. Olson at Hannah's shoulder. "She's been sizing us up all afternoon."

"She's an angel," Hannah said. "I'm so glad she's finally here! But what will her name be?"

"She's Naomi Mae," announced Rachel. "But that's kind of a mouthful for a little one. For now, we'll just call her Mae."

"Happy Birthday, Baby Mae," whispered Hannah to the little bundle, whose eyes had closed again.

"Happy Birthday, Aunt Hannah," smiled Rachel.

Chapter Eight

WEDDING DAY

Miss Devine and Mr. Moore were married one week after school recessed for summer vacation.

Miss Devine had come through the months of preparations in relative serenity. Her aunt had worried for both of them. "June can be hot," Mrs. Martin-Mitchell fretted during the days before the wedding. "You'll roast in that gown, Delia. And the ice cream sherbet will melt."

The twelfth of June dawned cool, which was a relief to Mrs. Martin-Mitchell. But she soon found a new worry. "Look at those clouds," she frowned, staring out the window of the largest upstairs room at Pine Craig. "It's sure to rain. Why didn't we think of this before?"

"It's not going to rain, Aunt Helen. I don't know what's come over you recently. I've never seen you like this."

"Helping plan a wedding is a big responsibility,"

said Mrs. Martin-Mitchell. "I'm more nervous about yours than I was about my own. Do you suppose the girls will be here soon? It's almost time!"

Fortunately, the six flower girls all arrived early. Mrs. Martin-Mitchell fluttered around, passing out the gowns.

"Let's see, you're in yellow, Polly."

"No, Ma'am," responded Polly politely. "Blue is my color." Winnie giggled and elbowed Polly. Polly responded with a frown.

"Do you need help, Sister dear?" called a voice to Mrs. Martin-Mitchell from the doorway. It was Miss Devine's mother, who had arrived that week on the train from Philadelphia with her husband. "How lovely you girls will look!" she exclaimed.

Mrs. Devine helped sort the dresses. Before long, the flower-girl rainbow was arranged. Floral hoops were given to each child and, in a rainbow whirl, they were shepherded to the waiting carriage.

"I wish we'd had a chance to see Miss Devine before we left," Beth said. "I guess her gown is going to be a surprise."

There had been a rehearsal at St. Luke's the previous day. Hannah had recommended the flower girls walk down the aisle of the church according to the "correct" order of the color spectrum. Miss Devine had approved. Mr. Moore said it was a fine thing that Hannah knew the proper order. "I wish more children were as interested in science as you are," he remarked with a grin.

Now, standing in the church vestibule with the music about to begin, the girls had the jitters. Miss Devine's Aunt Helen swept into church wearing a tan satin dress with trailing skirts. She had left her anxieties at the house.

"You look calm, cool, and collected, Mrs. Martin-Mitchell," Beth commented.

"I'm feeling much better, thank you," Mrs. Martin-Mitchell confided. "It's such a relief to have the big moment here at last."

The organist began to play and the flower girls started up the aisle: first Beth, then Winnie, Ellie, Maggie, Polly, and Hannah. They walked slowly, holding their hoops of flowers at their sides.

At the front of the chapel, the girls stepped up onto the curving steps, three on each side, and turned to face the congregation. They tried to look very solemn. Mr. Moore, standing by the steps, winked at them.

Stirring chords from the organ signaled that the bride was about to come down the aisle. A collective gasp of admiration went up when Miss Devine entered on the arm of her father.

A long veil descended from a crown of flowers and ivy on her head. Her golden-brown hair was dressed in loose ringlets which coiled gracefully on her neck. Rows of pleats and ruffles, ending in satin bows, ran down the sides and front of her white silk taffeta dress. The bodice was trimmed with white lace and tiny white rosebuds–real ones. The wrists of the dress were tied with satin bows, rosebuds, and sprigs of green ivy.

The flower girls were entranced as Miss Devine came up the aisle. Beth peeked at Mr. Moore, who looked as though he were seeing a vision. Miss Devine was radiant as she took his hand.

After the ceremony, a flower-decked carriage carried the newly-married couple to Pine Craig, where an elaborate reception awaited. The six girls rode back in a larger carriage, also decorated with flowers.

The wedding party met in the Octagon where Mrs. Martin-Mitchell was wringing her hands once again.

"What's the trouble, Aunt Helen?" the new Mrs.

Moore asked. "Things are going beautifully, thanks to your careful planning."

"But did you see that western sky? I'm sure it's going to rain after all. What will we do? The tables are all set. Oh, those beautiful cakes out in the rain!" Mrs. Martin-Mitchell looked as though she were about to cry.

"It does seem as though the wind has picked up," offered Winnie.

Maggie glared at her. "Shh! You're going to make Mrs. Martin-Mitchell feel worse."

"Let's go take a look," urged Ellie.

The flower girls turned to the outside door of the Octagon. "It doesn't feel like rain," said Hannah hopefully, stepping out.

The grounds of Pine Craig were flawlessly beautiful. The topiary rose bushes–yellow, pink, and orange–had all come into bloom just a few days before. On their long stems were pink, peach, yellow, blue, mint, and violet ribbons tied together in gay bunches.

Long tables set outside the Octagon held a buffet of hot and cold dishes. One held the towering white wedding cake, trimmed in a rainbow of pastel roses. It would be served with rainbow sherbet ice cream.

Round tables, draped in white linen tablecloths, had been arranged around the small pond. And on every table stood a miniature wedding cake. Each small three-tiered cake was iced in a different rainbow shade. Maggie admired a cake frosted in mint green. "It matches my dress!" she laughed.

The guests were beginning to arrive, and the bridal couple came out to admire their lovely reception.

"Mrs. Martin-Mitchell," Beth cried suddenly. "Come out, quickly!"

"What is it Beth?" asked Mr. Moore.

"The storm," she said. "It's passed off to the south. And look what it left behind." She pointed up to the sky.

They all gazed up to the southern sky where, over the trees, gleamed a beautiful rainbow.

"Wow," said Maggie. "You weren't kidding when you said this would be a rainbow wedding!"